Copyright © 2002 by Michael Neugebauer Verlag,
an imprint of Nord-Süd Verlag AG, Gossau Zürich, Switzerland
First published in Switzerland under the title *Pauli, Hilfe, ein Gespenst!*
English translation copyright © 2002 by North-South Books Inc., New York

First published in the United States, Great Britain, Canada,
Australia, and New Zealand in 2002 by North-South Books,
an imprint of Nord-Süd Verlag AG, Gossau Zürich, Switzerland.

Distributed in the United States by North-South Books Inc., New York.

Library of Congress Cataloging-in-Publication Data is available.
A CIP catalogue record for this book is available from The British Library.
ISBN 0-7358-1687-5 (trade edition) 10 9 8 7 6 5 4 3 2 1
ISBN 0-7358-1688-3 (library edition) 10 9 8 7 6 5 4 3 2 1
Printed in Italy

For more information about our books, and the authors and artists
who create them, visit our web site: www.northsouth.com

Davy, Help!
It's a Ghost!

Brigitte Weninger
Illustrated by Eve Tharlet

Translated by J. Alison James

A MICHAEL NEUGEBAUER BOOK
NORTH-SOUTH BOOKS
NEW YORK/LONDON

One evening Mother and Father Rabbit wanted to go out. Davy and his brothers and sisters were going to stay at home all by themselves. Big brother Dan was in charge.

"Will you be able to get to sleep on your own?" asked Mother, worried.

"Yes, Mother."

"Remember, don't let anyone in."

"Yes, Mother."

"Are you sure that you won't be afraid?"

"Yes, Mother."

"You've asked us ten times already," Davy said. "We'll be fine."

"Davy is right," Father Rabbit said. "Dan is old enough now to keep an eye on things. He is very responsible."

"Yippie! Alone at last!" Davy cried.
Joyfully the children played all the games they
could think of—Toss the Bunny, Pillow Fight,
and Leaf Lotto. They gobbled up the snacks
that Mother had left for them and drank
all the raspberry juice.
"Oh, it's so much fun to be at home alone!"
Davy said.

At last, baby Dinah fell asleep on the floor. Daisy and Donny rubbed their eyes. "Do you think we ought to go to bed?" asked their big brother, Dan.

"I guess so," said Davy, yawning.

The Rabbit children brushed their teeth and slipped under the covers. "Good night, Dan. Good night, Donny. Good night, Daisy. Good night, Dinah."
"Good night, Davy!" they said back.
Soon all was still.

"HELP!!! A GHOST!"

Daisy stood up in her bed, her face as white as chalk.

"What? Where?" All the children were wide awake.

"There—there it is! It flew past the window," said Daisy.

Trembling, the children watched the window.
"Dinah sleep with Davy," the baby said.
Davy's heart was thudding in his throat. They all squeezed into Donny's bed. Huddling together, they listened in the darkness—*crackle* and *rattle* at the window; *scritch scratch knock* at the door.

"The ghost is out there,"
whispered Daisy.
"It could be the wind,"
said Dan.
"Do you want to go and see?"
asked Donny.
But Dan shook his head.

"Are we going to sit here all night being scared?" asked Davy.

"What else can we do?" said Donny.

Davy thought hard. Suddenly he jumped up:

"I know! We can scare away the ghost!"

"Are you out of your mind?" cried the others. "The ghost would rip you to pieces. You can't go out there!"
"Who said that I would go outside?" asked Davy.
"The important thing is that the ghost doesn't come in here!" Then he told them his idea.

Brave Davy was the first out of bed. He ran and turned on the light. Then all the Rabbit children went to work.

They took the broom from the corner and pulled a sheet off the bed. They plumped a pillow into the shape of a ball. Davy painted a scary face on a piece of paper. Before they knew it, a gruesome Rabbit Monster stared out at the night.

"There," cried Davy satisfied. "That ghost won't dare come in the window now."

"But what if it comes in the door?" asked Daisy.
"Uh oh, you're right. We need a second monster," Davy said.

Finally all was done.
The door and the window were well guarded.
Tired, the children crawled back in bed.
"Sleep well," said Davy quietly.
"I sure hope so," murmured Dan.

Crackle and *rattle* at the window; *scritch scratch knock* at the door. The doorknob clicked. Davy sat straight up in bed, his heart pounding wildly. He heard the door squeak open slowly.

"HELP!!! A GHOST!"

The monster guarding the door crashed to the floor!

"What is this?" a voice spluttered. It was Father! The light
  flashed on.

"Oh, Father! Mother! You're home!" cried the children.

"There was a ghost outside. But Davy had this great idea
  to scare it with the Rabbit Monster!"

"That was clever," said Mother.
"Yes, you children really know how to
take care of yourselves," praised Father.

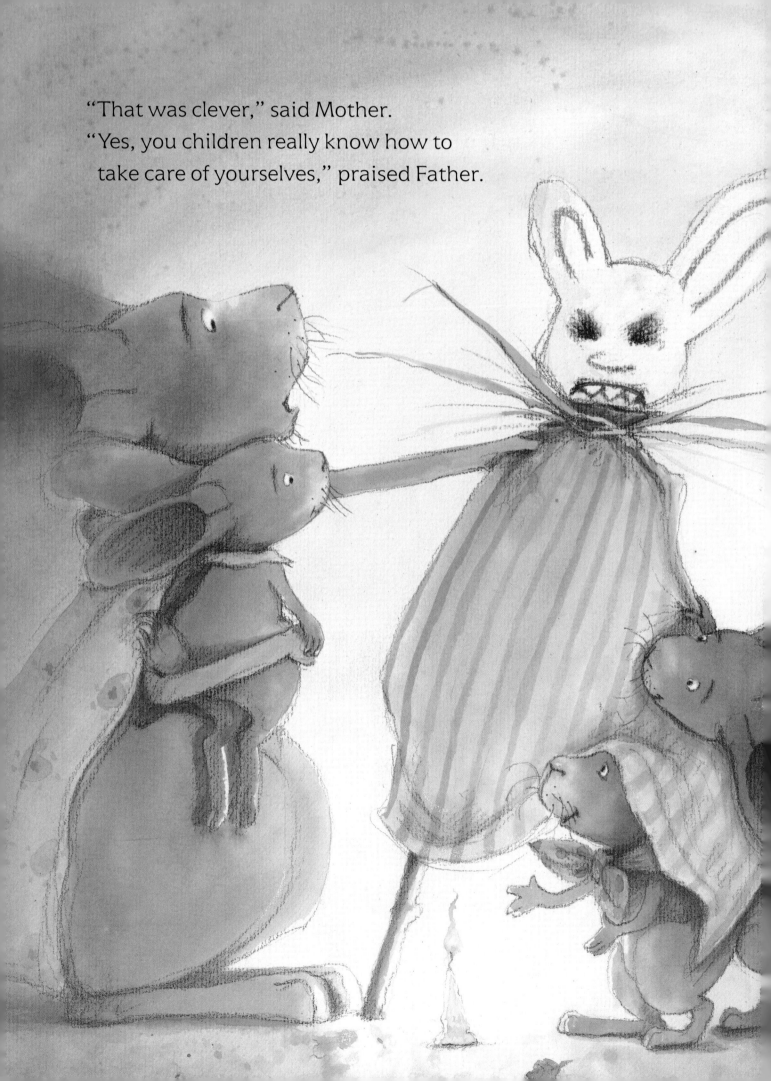

"Dinah sleep with Mama!" begged the baby.

"Of course, my darling. I'll stay in your room tonight."

"I don't know," said Father, looking out of the window. "What about me? What if the ghost is still creeping around outside? What if it comes in my window?"

Davy ran to him and pulled on his arm. "Come, Father. I have another good idea . . ."

"Tonight both of you can sleep in our room!"